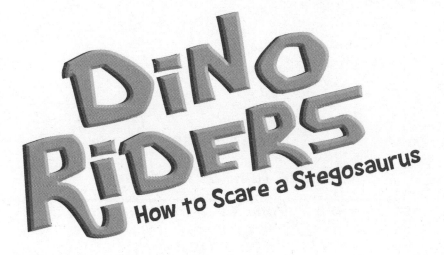

How to Scare a Stegosaurus

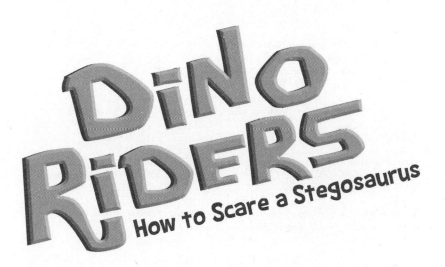

DINO RIDERS

How to Scare a Stegosaurus

Will Dare

sourcebooks
jabberwocky

Published by Sourcebooks Jabberwocky, an imprint of Sourcebooks, Inc.
P.O. Box 4410, Naperville, Illinois 60567–4410
(630) 961-3900
Fax: (630) 961-2168
sourcebooks.com

Library of Congress Cataloging-in-Publication Data

Names: Dare, Will, author.
Title: How to scare a stegosaurus / Will Dare.
Description: Naperville, Illinois : Sourcebooks Jabberwocky, [2018] | Series: Dino riders ; [6] | Summary: While the sheriff is away, crooked, businessman Malachi Wilks and his stegosaurus workers try to build a railroad through Trihorn Valley, with only Josh and his friends standing in his way.
Identifiers: LCCN 2018030653 | (pbk. : alk. paper)
Subjects: | CYAC: Dinosaurs--Fiction. | Stegosaurus--Fiction. | Swindlers and swindling--Fiction. | Railroads--Fiction.
Classification: LCC PZ7.1.D32 Hnm 2018 | DDC [E]--dc23
LC record available at https://lccn.loc.gov/2018030653

Source of Production: Versa Press, East Peoria, Illinois, United States
Date of Production: September 2018
Run Number: 5013138

Printed and bound in the United States of America.
VP 10 9 8 7 6 5 4 3 2 1

With special thanks to Jonny Leighton.

The Lost Plains

here be dinosaurs

N
W E
S

Scaly Point Settlement

more Wandering Mountains

Wandering Mountains

Roaring Jaws Valley

Cold Fear Forest

Scratchclaw Swamps

Trihorn Settlement

Trihorn Road

Sanders' Ranch

Iguanodon Plains

Loneheart Lakes

CHAPTER 1

'm *hungrrry!*" a voice drawled. "My stomach is churning like two rats in a sack!"

Josh Sanders looked up from under the wide brim of his hat. He and his best friends had been out on the Sanders' family ranch all day long, herding iguanodons across the Lost Plains. Now, the sun was beginning to droop toward the horizon, the air was starting to chill, bellies were beginning to rumble, and butts were getting sore in their saddles.

"Not long now, Sam," Josh said. "We're almost done."

"Yeah," Abi agreed. "Try to ignore those rats. There's just a few more iguanodons over the river. Once we round those up, we can head back into Trihorn Settlement."

Sam sighed. The three friends and their dinosaurs began crossing the river that separated Josh's family land from the rest of the plains. Josh sat on his muscly triceratops, Charge. Sam and Abi were on their quick-footed gallimimuses, Nickel and Fire.

"I suppose I'll just have to make do with these," Sam said, rummaging around in the pockets of his waistcoat. With a flourish, he pulled out a string of candy beads, a couple of hard candies, a paper bag full of Finton O'Malley's Fun Time Fudge, a fistful of licorice whips, and a packet of Pterodactyl Tongue-Sizzler Candy Rocks.

Josh let out a belly laugh.

Abi just rolled her eyes. "And that's not enough to keep you from being hungry?" she asked.

"I'm a growing boy!" Sam whined. "I need this much food to, you know, dodge T. rexes and fight velociraptors and stuff."

"Uh-huh." Josh laughed. "How about dodging this?"

Josh yanked on his reins. Charge knew exactly what to do. The giant triceratops reared up on his back legs, then brought his front legs crashing down into the river, right by Sam and Nickel. The water splashed upward and covered Sam from head to toe.

Josh and Abi burst out laughing. Sam shook off the stinky mud and water. For a second, his brow furrowed in anger, but then he couldn't help but laugh too.

"Well, fine," he said, grinning. "No candy for you." He crammed a fistful of fudge into his mouth and then shoved the rest of his wares back into his waistcoat pocket.

The three friends splashed through the river that marked the boundary of the Sanders' ranch. Their dinosaurs happily waded farther into the water until it splashed halfway up their legs. As the current quickened around them, though, Abi yanked on her reins. Her dinosaur, Fire, stopped in her tracks, and Abi held her hand up to her ear.

"Do you fellas hear that?" she asked.

Josh and Sam brought their dinos to a halt and pricked up their ears. There was a definite rumbling noise coming from somewhere.

"Is that your stomach, Sam?" Josh asked.

Sam shook his head, his cheeks bulging with fudge. "S'not me!" he managed to say.

"Then what the—" Josh began. But he didn't get to finish his question. Soon, the answer was practically staring him in the face—and filling his nostrils. The rumbling grew louder and louder until it became a deafening roar. The smell rose like a mixture of old cabbages and dirty laundry. Up ahead was not one, not two, but *five* huge dinosaurs. And they were all coming their way.

"Stegosauruses!" Josh cried. "They're heading right for us!"

Josh yanked on his reins and swerved out of the way. Sam and Abi crouched low in their saddles. However, there was nothing they could do to avoid the rampaging dinos. The first of the stegosauruses was on them in a flash. The huge beast must have been thirty feet long. It had strong, kite-shaped armor all the way down its back and a spiky tail that looked like it could take down a T. rex. Its stinky, leathery skin covered bulging muscles that would all too easily crush you if you got too close. It let out a deep bellow, as if it were telling Josh and his friends to get out of the way.

"Holy ghosts!" Josh cried. "Stick together, guys!"

Josh, Sam, and Abi huddled close, making themselves as big an obstacle as possible. The stego crashed into the water, sending mud and muck up all around them. Josh readied his lasso to flick at the beast. He lashed outward with the rope, stinging the dino on its leg. Luckily, it was just enough to make the dino dodge them, but they were still buffeted by its giant, muscly legs and completely drenched by the waves.

"Gah!" he cried. "Take that, you oversized lizard!"

Not all the stegos had riders, and they stumbled to and fro like giant, out-of-control toddlers. As one smaller stegosaurus crossed the river, Josh saw it was much more reluctant than the others. Its rider had to wrestle with the reins as the stego hesitated on the banks of the river, slip-sliding in the mud, before finally

charging ahead into the water and barreling past the three of them.

"Jeez!" Sam shouted. "That was a bit close, wasn't it?"

Abi breathed heavily. "Just a bit!" she agreed. "Those smelly stegos nearly pounded us into paste!"

Josh felt his heartbeat return to normal, and his fear changed into confusion. *What in the Lost Plains are five huge stegosauruses doing speeding across my family's land?* he wondered. Normally, the big brutes were only used for pulling stagecoaches. But there were no coaches in sight. And anyway, no one would ever let the coaches move that fast or across a raging river!

He peered farther into the distance and saw that the stegos weren't the last of the dinos. There were other riders coming up behind them. A group of men on gallimimuses and ankylosaurs trooped across the river too. They carried sacks on their backs, and their dinosaurs' saddlebags were overflowing with tools: hammers, pickaxes, wrenches, and saws.

"Hey," Josh called up to one of the riders. "What are you lot up to? No one told us about a party of stegos trooping through here. You'll scare the iguanodons!"

The gruff-looking rider pulled up his steed and chucked something at Josh. Without so much as a word, he yanked his reins and was on his way.

"Pfft!" Josh said. "Some people."

Abi nodded. "But what is it, Josh? What did he throw you?"

Josh held in his hands a piece of rolled-up paper. He broke the wax seal, unraveled the parchment, and scanned the words as quickly as possible. As his eyes darted across the page, his stomach did a flip, and his heart sank.

"Uh-oh," he said.

"What does it say?" Sam asked, bringing his dinosaur nearer.

Josh took a deep breath and read out the notice.

"'Wilks Enterprises hereby gives notice of a new development: a railroad that will connect the Lost Plains together. Demolition by stegosaurus starts immediately, by order of the local court.' And it's signed Malachi Wilks."

"Railroad? Demolition?" Sam gasped. "Where does it go?"

"That's the bad news," said Josh. "It goes right through the heart of Trihorn Settlement!"

CHAPTER 2

J osh, Sam, and Abi pulled up outside Trihorn's courthouse and tied up their dinos. It had only been a couple of days since the first stegosaurus wrecking crew had arrived in town, but the whole place was in chaos. Word had quickly spread about the plan to build a railroad right through Trihorn, and folks weren't happy. Malachi "Moneymaker" Wilks was well known around the Lost Plains for his shady business dealings—stealing gold during the Great Gold Rush of '75, trying to steal the Sanders' ranch from under Josh's family's noses—but this time, he'd taken the cake...*and* eaten it! Trihorn would be demolished if Wilks had his way, and people were determined to stop him.

The three friends made their way into the local courthouse and were hit by a wall of sound. The room was packed full of people: local store owners, reporters, and squawking microraptors and other small dinosaurs. Pretty much the whole of Trihorn was out in force. They'd use the law to stop mean old Wilks, and that'd be the end of him.

"Wilks doesn't stand a chance," Josh said.

"Once Judge Mathers sees all of us Trihorners here, he's sure to be on our side."

"I hope you're right," Sam said.

"Uh, guys," Abi said, a note of concern in her voice. "That's all well and good about Judge Mathers. But who's that?" Abi pointed to a stern-looking man who walked up to the podium at the front of the room.

An official called for order, and everyone turned to look his way. The man had cold, black eyes and an icy stare that could freeze a

T. rex in its paces. His face looked stony and miserable, as if he'd never smiled in his life, and his bulky frame could have been carved out of rock.

"Order in this here courthouse!" he boomed.

Josh blinked and stepped back. The other Trihorners stood to attention. This judge was not the easygoing Judge Mathers they were used to. This guy was terrifying.

"Where's Mathers?" one brave resident shouted from the crowd.

"I told Mathers to take a vacation," the judge drawled. "I am his superior, Judge Coldbody, from Scaly Point. I am here to hear the case of *Wilks vs. Trihorn*. And if anyone doesn't like it, they know where the door is."

Josh, Sam, and Abi were chilled to the bone. Coldbody was scary. But Josh still had hope. After all, Trihorn had a strong case. Unfortunately, the person making it was the new mayor, Gieronimous Dorkins, who had a habit of droning on and on and missing the point a bit.

Mayor Dorkins looked excited as he waddled up to the dock. He loved rallying a crowd with his wild stories, no matter how off the point they were. A bead of sweat dripped down his forehead, but his bristly mustache danced across his lip like a wriggly caterpillar. No matter the threat to Trihorn, Dorkins was going to enjoy his moment in the spotlight.

"Ladies and gentlemen and dinosaurs,"

Mayor Dorkins began in a loud voice. "How is everyone today? Roaring to go, I hope!"

The residents of Trihorn looked on, unimpressed. Dorkins seemed to think the future of Trihorn was a chance to do a one-man show.

"O-kay," he drawled. "Tough crowd. So, what are we talking about today? Ah yes. Wilks's railroad going through Trihorn. Bad thing. Terrible. Terrible. You know, I remember, it must have been back in '82, we used to have to carry our own carts across the plains. We hadn't even tamed the large dinosaurs yet. Terrible thing, really. I could tell you a thing or two about those days…"

Josh was wondering what Mayor Dorkins was going on about. So, too, were the other residents.

Abi piped up behind him. "Get on with it, Mayor Dorkins!" she shouted.

"Yeah," Sam agreed. "Tell him this railroad is not going through our town!"

The residents cheered in approval, and Mayor Dorkins seemed to remember that he wasn't telling a funny fireside story about the good old days.

"Oh yes, well," Dorkins continued. "The point is that this development is illegal. We all know Malachi Wilks is a crook. He doesn't own Trihorn. If we have to, we'll drive this man right outta town ourselves!"

At this, the room erupted in cheers. The wooden floor rumbled, and the windows shuddered with the noise.

Good old Dorkins, Josh thought. He was a rambler, but like all ramblers, he got somewhere in the end.

Judge Coldbody slammed on the table with his gavel. "That's quite enough of that ruckus in my courtroom," he boomed. "Now, Mr. Wilks, would you like to say a few words?"

At the front of the courtroom, Josh saw the familiar spindly figure of Malachi Wilks take the podium. He was wizened and old, but he still had a famously mean glint in his eyes. He wore fine fabrics and jewelry, but he obviously still wanted more. A malicious grin was spread across his face like butter over bread.

"It's simple, your honor," he began, smiling up at Coldbody like they were best friends.

"The railroad *is* coming to Trihorn, and, ahem, also, with a final stop up at Loneheart Mansion—"

"Wait a minute!" Josh shouted. "That's where Wilks lives."

"Yeah!" Sam added. "He's just using the railroad as his private taxi service!"

Coldbody caught them in an icy glare that made both Sam and Josh shut their mouths double-quick.

"As I was saying. The railroad *will* be going ahead for one very simple reason." At this, Wilks rummaged around in his pocket. He pulled out a piece of paper that had been folded into a tiny square. He gently unfolded it for everybody to see. "Contrary to what Mayor Dorkins says, the fact is, I *do* own Trihorn Settlement. So I can do as I please."

The room erupted into cries of disbelief. Josh, Sam, and Abi joined in the shouts. It couldn't be true. What was he talking about? How could one man own a whole town? Nobody had signed up for that. There had to be some mistake.

Judge Coldbody demanded order from the

rabble of residents once again. He took the parchment from Wilks and read it carefully. Then he showed the crowd the bottom of the document, signed by none other than Mayor Dorkins. Everyone reeled back in shock. Mayor Dorkins scrambled to explain.

"B-but," he said, peering at the document, "I thought that was the sign-up form for the Dino Circus. I've always thought I'd make a good clown..."

Wilks's smile got even wider, as if he knew he had poor Mayor Dorkins trapped. "That's funny," he said. "I've always seen you as a bit of a clown too."

Pros and Cons
of the Roaring Railroad

PROs	CONs
-Get to Wild Dino Springs in less than five hours!	-The wild dinosaurs at Wild Dino Springs tend to eat people.
-We could finally find out which is faster: steam train or velociraptor.	-Velociraptors don't tend to like races. They prefer clawing at people's heads.
-Wouldn't a train ride be fun?	-It would mean the end of the Trihorn Settlement...forever!

Josh's heart sank. Dorkins had been fooled. He'd certainly gotten what he wanted—he was most definitely a clown.

Coldbody banged his gavel on the table once more and dismissed the case. "Trihorn belongs to Mr. Wilks to do with as he wishes," he said. "The Roaring Railroad shall go ahead!"

T he next day, Josh, Sam, and Abi wandered
through Trihorn Settlement on their
dinosaurs. All three of them were feeling
glum. And angry.

"How can they do this?" Josh fumed. "Trihorn
has stood for years. And now they're bulldozing
it to make way for a railroad? It goes right from
Loneheart Mansion to Scaly Point Settlement.
And that will only be good for one man!"

Sam and Abi nodded in agreement. As if to rub salt in their wounds, a stegosaurus charged past with one of the bulldozing workers on top. The dinosaur kicked up a whole load of dust and soot from the main road, which set Josh off sneezing and rubbing his eyes.

Abi shielded her face. "These stegosauruses are a menace! And they stink. They're not supposed to charge around so fast."

"The smaller dinos are not much better!" Sam added. There must have been twenty of them coming through Trihorn that morning, a combination of gallimimuses and ankylosaurs. Each had a rider who carried saddlebags full of tools, either to begin laying the track or to demolish bits of Trihorn.

"Look," said Josh. "Even Mrs. Tumble is leaving…"

The group passed Mrs. Tumble's dino pet shop. She stocked everything from aquilopes to zephyrosauruses, but now she was letting the dino pets loose to make their own way in the world, and her shop was being boarded up. Lizards scurried across the street, and larger, flying microraptors took to the sky. As colorful as parrots, the microraptors always squawked like them too. They'd even managed to pick up a few words from humans, which they repeated on a loop. One of them perched on a telegraph pole and squawked "Railroad, railroad" until Josh was tempted to scare it away with his lasso.

Trundling down the road came something

even more annoying: Malachi Wilks's nephew Amos and his pal Arthur. Amos sat on top of his dinosaur, Clubber, and seemed to swagger as he did so.

"Looks like my uncle got his railroad, dweebs," he boasted proudly. "He always gets what he wants in the end."

"Yeah," Arthur said. "H-h-how do you feel about that?"

Josh balled his fists in anger. "Your uncle only got his way because Judge Coldbody was on his side. Anyone could see that. And besides, the fight isn't over. We're going to save Trihorn Settlement, no matter what it takes. Aren't we, guys?"

Sam and Abi nodded in agreement. Amos still

The businesses of Trihorn County that will be no more

Mary Schumer Dinosaur Groomer

"Make your dino look fab-u-lous!"

Trihorn Yarn Store

"When your dino needs a winter scarf."

Mystic Ella, Fortune Teller

"Find out what the stars have in store for you and your dinosaur!"

grinned his horrible grin, but right then, the microraptor that had been perched above took off. Midflight, it swooped down, screeched "railroad, railroad," and then pooped right on Amos's head. Some of it even splashed onto Arthur too. Josh, Sam, and Abi burst out laughing.

"Ewww, gross!" Amos cried. "Did you train that raptor to do that, Sanders?"

"No!" Josh said through his laughter. "But I wish I had!"

Amos wiped the poo off his head. "Urgh, come on, Arthur. Let's go. We don't want to be around these losers any longer."

"You're the one with microraptor poo on your head, Amos." Sam giggled. "I'm pretty sure that that makes you the loser!"

36

Amos and Arthur turned furiously and rode off down Main Street. The microraptor followed them the whole way like a bad cloud.

"That's one way to get rid of them," Abi said with a laugh.

"Yeah," Josh agreed. "I wish we'd thought of using them years ago! We could have gotten rid of them for good. But if only we had a way of getting rid of those too."

Josh pointed down the street. A giant stegosaurus and his rider were already demolishing the old tavern. Bits of wood and metal went flying through the air as the building began to disintegrate before their eyes. The huge dinosaurs were using their spiky tails to clobber the walls. The bulldozing crew followed behind, using pickaxes and hammers to tear down what was left.

Just then, one of the giant stegosauruses took a step back into the street—all the better to run and smash into the building some more. But instead, it accidentally barreled straight into a water main on Main Street. The weight of the dinosaur broke it completely, sending plumes of water soaring into the air. The stegosaurus took a step back in fright and reared up on its back legs.

When the stegosaurus bent its giant neck downward and saw the pools of water at its feet, it did another double take and jumped back in fright. Its rider struggled to restrain it as it stampeded down Main Street. Sam and Abi had to jump to the side once more to avoid being trampled by its giant bulk.

"Whoa," said Sam. "What's up with that guy?

"I dunno," said Abi. "It was like he got stung on the butt by a couple hundred bees!"

But Josh had a different thought. He was starting to put two and two together. First, there was the stego that tried to jump over the river but wasn't having any of it. Then, there was this stego that jumped back at the sight of water.

"Guys," he said triumphantly. "I've got it! The stegosauruses are afraid of water."

Sam and Abi nodded in realization. "That explains it!" they both agreed.

"And now we've got the upper hand," Josh said proudly.

"How do you work that one out, dino rider?" Sam asked.

"Because," Josh began, "now I've got a plan!"

CHAPTER

4

S am's fingers whizzed through the giant old Dino Directory like there was no tomorrow. Every dinosaur in the Lost Plains was in the huge, leather-bound book, so it took a bit of time. It wasn't even in alphabetical order. Some genius had decided to list the dinosaurs in order of ferociousness, which meant finding the stegosaurus took ages.

"You boys nearly done over there?" Mr. O'Riley

shouted. The post office was about to close. In fact, the post office was about to close *forever*, and Mr. O'Riley wasn't waiting around any longer than he had to. "You young 'uns take much longer, and the dinosaurs will go extinct!"

"Ha ha! Yeah, good one, Mr. O'Riley," Josh said and laughed. "That'll be the day." He turned back to Sam anxiously. "You found anything yet?"

"Just a minute," said Sam. He flicked past megalosaurus, torosaurus, and protoceratops. He was just beginning to give up hope when he finally found something. "Yes! That's it. *Stegosaurus stenops—*"

"Never mind its fancy name!" Josh cried. "What does the entry say?"

Protoceratops

~~~~~~~~~~~~~~~~~~~~~~~~~~
~~~~~~~~~~~~~~~~~~~~~~~~~~
~~~~~~~~~~~~~~~~~~~~~~~~~~
~~~~~~~~~~~~~~~~~~~~~~~~~~
~~~~~~~~~~~~~~~~~~~~~~~~~~

Torosaurus

~~~~~~~~~~~~~~~~~~~~~~~~~~
~~~~~~~~~~~~~~~~~~~~~~~~~~
~~~~~~~~~~~~~~~~~~~~~~~~~~
~~~~~~~~~~~~~~~~~~~~~~~~~~
~~~~~~~~~~~~~~~~~~~~~~~~~~
~~~~~~~~~~~~~~~~~~~~~~~~~~
~~~~~~~~~~~~~~~~~~~~~~~~~~

Megalosaurus

~~~~~~~~~~~~~~~~~~~~~~~~~~
~~~~~~~~~~~~~~~~~~~~~~~~~~
~~~~~~~~~~~~~~~~~~~~~~~~~~
~~~~~~~~~~~~~~~~~~~~~~~~~~
~~~~~~~~~~~~~~~~~~~~~~~~~~
~~~~~~~~~~~~~~~~~~~~~~~~~~
~~~~~~~~~~~~~~~~~~~~~~~~~~

Sam scanned the page. "Big, brutish, twenty-nine-and-a-half feet long. Up to seven tons in weight. Stegos are large and bumbling and good for pulling stagecoaches and carrying out occasional demolition work. It says they can be nervous and skittish creatures, but it doesn't say anything about being afraid of water—"

"Well, that's it!" Josh said, completely ignoring the bit where water wasn't mentioned. "They're nervous and skittish. They've got to be afraid of something, right? So it must be water that they're afraid of. We saw it with our very own eyes."

"Well, I dunno," Sam began. "We saw something all right."

But Sam didn't get a chance to finish.

 44

Josh punched the air triumphantly. He dragged Sam out of the post office and back out onto Main Street, waving good-bye to Mr. O'Riley, who finally got to close his shop.

"Tell Abi to meet us on the corner of Main Street and Dino Avenue first thing tomorrow morning," Josh said, the excitement rising in his voice.

"Why?" Sam asked. "What are we doing? And where are you going now?"

"I've got work to do, my friend," Josh said proudly. "You just wait and see!"

Stego-Scaring Ideas

1.) Trick the stegosauruses into going down a water slide.

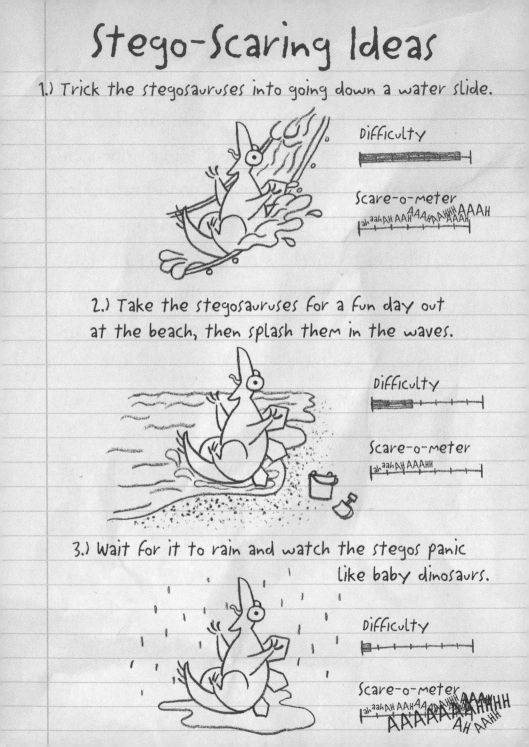

Difficulty

Scare-o-meter

ah aah AH AAH AAAh AHH AAAH

2.) Take the stegosauruses for a fun day out at the beach, then splash them in the waves.

Difficulty

Scare-o-meter

ah aah AH AAAHH

3.) Wait for it to rain and watch the stegos panic like baby dinosaurs.

Difficulty

Scare-o-meter

ah aah AH AAAH AA AHH AAAHHH
AAAAAAAHHH
AH AAHH

The next morning, Sam and Abi raced down Main Street just as the sun was beginning to rise over the nearby hills. They still had no idea what Josh had been planning, but they were about to find out.

"Wait a doggone minute," Abi said as they approached her family's grocery store on the corner of Main and Dino. "Is that Josh? On the roof of my grocery store?"

Sam's mouth hung slack. He could only nod in agreement. It certainly was Josh on top of Abi's family's grocery store roof. Abi looked like she was going to blow her top.

"Hey, you!" she shouted, her cheeks pink. "What in the Lost Plains are you doing up there!"

Josh smiled heartily and put his finger to his

lips. "Shh." He laughed. "You'll wake the whole of Trihorn. Anyway, isn't it obvious?"

Sam and Abi looked up. Josh was perched on top of the one-story building with a giant hose gripped tightly in his hands. The other end of the hose was attached to a water main down below at street level.

"So this is your big plan, huh?" said Sam. "You're going to give the stinky stegosauruses a shower? If I'd known that, I wouldn't have got washed this morning, and I'd have joined in too!"

"No, not a shower, you doofus," Josh said. "They're scared of water. So I'm gonna frighten them out of this town for good!"

Sam and Abi shook their heads as if to say

that Josh was nuts. But just then, the group heard the first rumblings of stegosauruses making their way down Main Street for today's bulldozing.

"Abi!" Josh shouted. "Quick! You get up here with me."

"Oh, you've got to be kidding me," she said.

"No, I am not," Josh said. "And Sam, you stay down there. When I give you the signal, bust that water main."

"B-but…" Sam began.

"Just do it!" Josh demanded. "We're saving Trihorn, remember?"

Abi reluctantly tied up Fire and made her way around to the back of the shop, where iron ladders hung down the side of the wall. She clambered up them and joined Josh, who was now lying flat on his belly, clutching the hose. She lay down beside him. Below, Sam was standing by the water main, ready for action.

"You know this is a dumb idea, right?" said Abi.

"No way," said Josh. "This is what a real dino rider would do. Just like T-Bill. Just like Rona Rawfoot."

Josh had his Lost Plains heroes, and he would always do what he could to be just like them.

Just then, the first of the stego crews trundled into view. Four of the beasts, with their riders on top, were making their way to work, getting ready to demolish the bank in the center of the street. Josh lined up the hose carefully,

and just when the dinosaurs were in the right place, he let it rip.

"Now, Sam!" he cried.

Below, Sam yanked on the lever that controlled the mains. There was a gurgle and a rushing sound as the surging water made its way up through the hose and then out. Josh released the catch, and he and Abi hung on to the wild thing for dear life.

Water gushed out onto Main Street, right at the stegosauruses, coming at them like an iron ball out of a cannon. The riders on top of the stegos shrieked, and the stegos themselves stepped back.

"Yee-haw!" Josh whooped. "Now we got 'em!"

The whole of Main Street was turning into a

mess of water and dirt. The riders down below still hollered, but the stegos seemed to be going about their normal business. Now that the initial scare was over, they weren't bothered.

"Did it work?" Abi asked.

Josh wasn't sure. They'd definitely managed to annoy the bulldozing crew, but he wasn't sure if that was enough. Just at that moment, he saw another couple of figures come down the swampy street: Malachi Wilks and Judge Coldbody.

"Oh jeez," Josh said. "Who called *them*?"

"I dunno, but quick," said Abi. "Duck down."

But it was too late. The lead bulldozer was chatting with Wilks and Coldbody. Then he lifted his arm and pointed straight up at where Josh and Abi were hiding.

CHAPTER

5

Josh and Abi climbed down the iron steps to face the mean-eyed judge and the crooked businessman. Together with Sam, they squared up to Coldbody and Wilks. Quickly, the lawman strode over to them, fists clenched like he meant business.

"I ought to chuck you in prison and throw away the keys," said Judge Coldbody, quivering with rage. "Look what a mess you've made of Main Street."

"What does it matter?" Josh spat, firmly holding his ground and finding his courage. "You're just going to destroy it anyway. We might as well flood the whole street."

At this, a wicked grin spread across Malachi Wilks's face. "You may be on to something, young whippersnapper. Perhaps I should have done that in the first place. It would have saved me all this trouble."

Josh, Abi, and Sam all grumbled. Here was Malachi Wilks, building an entire railroad completely for his own benefit, destroying the settlement, and he was taking pleasure in it as well.

The stegosaurus crew was getting back to work. The dinos were smashing their way through another building, and the wreckers were tearing down whatever they could find. Josh's heart sank.

"And if you think the railroad can be stopped, you have another think coming," Wilks continued. "There are *even more* stegosauruses arriving at noon tomorrow. Twenty, in fact. What you see here now is merely an advance party. What you see tomorrow will take your breath away. And they'll take Trihorn with it."

"Now run along," said Coldbody, "or I'll have to get the sheriff involved."

Coldbody and Wilks sauntered off down the street, not a care in the world. As the water flooded away down the street, Josh, Sam, and Abi had nothing else to do but make their way back to where their dinosaurs were tied up. They all hung their heads and walked in silence. Josh's plan hadn't worked. The stegosauruses weren't bothered by the water. If they couldn't stop just a handful of them, how on earth were they supposed to stop even more stegosauruses that arrived tomorrow?

"That's it, then," Sam said glumly. "The end of Trihorn Settlement as we know it."

"Yup," Abi agreed. "Me and my folks will have to pack up and move the grocery store somewhere else. Maybe across the Wandering Mountains. Perhaps we'll end up in Scaly Point Settlement. I hope they like their vegetables!"

Josh scuffed the ground. He'd lived in Trihorn his whole life. His family had owned the ranch for generations. How were they supposed to just up and leave? Where would they even go? He fumed at the injustice of the whole situation. He stopped in the street and then began to turn back.

"Hey!" Sam shouted. "Where are you going?"

"The dinos are this way!" Abi shouted.

"I'm not getting Charge," Josh said. "I'm going to give Wilks a piece of my mind!"

Abi and Sam turned and tried to catch up with Josh.

"No!" said Abi. "That's just going to make things worse."

But Josh didn't care. He'd already tried to get rid of the dinosaurs. But maybe if he could show Wilks how much he cared about Trihorn and his ranch, he might be persuaded to stop destroying it.

Sam and Abi caught up with Josh, and together they turned down Horntooth Avenue. Josh was quickly turning his head left and right in the busy street, but he couldn't see Coldbody or Wilks anywhere. He asked a woman if she'd seen them, and she quickly nodded her assent.

"Well," she began, "if you mean that weedy, nasty nuisance with the big burly bloke with a butt for a face, then yes. They went thataway." She pointed down a narrow side street.

Josh, Abi, and Sam thanked her and made their way in the direction she'd pointed.

"Are you sure this is a good idea?" Sam asked. "What if he brings even more stegosauruses?

What if he brings them today? Just to teach us a lesson."

"Then at least we'll know we've done something," said Josh. "Instead of rolling over like, like...like Charge when he wants a belly rub!"

They continued down the dusty alleyway until they caught sight of Wilks and Judge Coldbody. However, something made Josh stop. Instead of continuing down the alleyway, the judge and the businessman had stopped and seemed to be conferring over something.

"Quick, duck down," said Josh. He pulled his two friends down behind a garbage can.

"What are they up to?" Abi wondered as they strained to listen. "What is that?"

The children peered forward. Malachi Wilks

was taking something out of the inside of his jacket. The three friends could just about hear what he said.

"And there's more where that came from," Wilks hissed. "Just make sure nothing else goes wrong. We don't want those kids poking their noses into other people's business, right?"

"All right, all right," Coldbody said. His voice sounded much less mean and scary. In fact, it was like he was the one taking orders from Wilks. "I'm already doing it, aren't I?"

It looked like Wilks was passing the judge an envelope. Coldbody went to snatch it, but as he did, it fell to the ground and spilled its contents all over the ground.

"They're dino dollar bills!" Josh gasped.

"They must be worth hundreds," said Sam. "Maybe even thousands!"

Coldbody quickly grabbed up the dusty money from the ground and stuffed it back in the envelope. He safely tucked it into his pocket, and the two men shook hands. They walked together down to the end of the alley, then went their separate ways.

"That sneaky, no-good, dirty ratbag!" said Abi. "Judge Coldbody is being bribed! No wonder the railroad is going through without a fuss."

A smile swiftly crossed Josh's face. "That means Trihorn is saved!"

CHAPTER 6

The next day, Josh, Sam, and Abi rode out early, determined to get to the court-house before the wrecking crew got there first. Josh was excited. He'd seen no-good Malachi Wilks bribing Judge Coldbody with his own two eyes. Once everyone in Trihorn knew about it, the settlement would be saved, and there would be no more railroad.

The three friends tied up their dinosaurs

outside and made their way into the court-room. The room was quieter than it had been before. The only people left were a few small-time crooks, the last cases to be held in the courthouse. But there was still a sheriff there and a few people watching from the gallery. Judge Coldbody was hearing a case when they walked in.

"Ahem," he coughed. "And what do you squirts think you are doing here? Can't you see that we're busy with *adult* things that are *no* concern of yours? You should run along. Quickly, now."

Josh stepped up proudly. All eyes were on him. Normally, he'd be nervous, but right now, he didn't feel worried at all. Everyone in

Trihorn needed to know what a crook the judge was. And the best way to do it was right to Judge Coldbody's face.

"I'll tell you what *is* a concern of ours," Josh said bravely. "Bribery!"

At this, the few other people in the court-house began to murmur. They didn't have any clue what Josh was talking about, but he could see that Judge Coldbody shifted slightly in his seat. Everyone was waiting to hear what else the kids had to tell them.

"That's right," Sam said. "We saw Judge Coldbody and Malachi Wilks in the alley just off Horntooth Avenue yesterday."

"You bet we did," Abi added. "Malachi Wilks was giving the judge money. And lots of it!"

The murmurs in the crowd turned to grumbles. Then they turned to angry shouts when they realized what this meant. The crowd started demanding answers, yelling up at Judge Coldbody.

"Whaddya say to this?" one angry resident shouted.

"Are you in Malachi's pocket?" asked another.

Judge Coldbody looked a little shocked at first, but then he regained his composure. He straightened his hat and adjusted his expensive-looking bow tie.

"No," he said simply. "This is a false allegation by a bunch of known hoodlums. Just yesterday, they completely flooded Main Street. How can they possibly be taken seriously? Unless, of course," he said with a smirk, "you have some sort of evidence for this? A photograph perhaps? An adult who can verify this disgraceful story?"

Josh, Sam, and Abi looked at each other. All they had was their word. They didn't think about evidence. They knew what they saw, and surely that was enough? Besides, no one could just take a photograph in the street; photographs were for fancy, rich people and had to be done in special studios.

"Erm..." Josh muttered. "But..."

The judge gave the three of them an icy stare. The people in the courtroom sighed. "I'll take that as a no. There's obviously not one shred of proof. Frankly, you lot ought to get out of my courtroom before I put you in handcuffs."

The crowd continued to murmur, not knowing who to believe. Josh had assumed that the assembled Trihorners would believe them, but if there was no proof, the sheriff couldn't do anything.

Suddenly though, there came a familiar, deep thudding noise. The stegosauruses were back. Everyone could recognize their footsteps of doom now. Josh rushed to the window. As he peered through the pane, he could see that Wilks had been right the previous day. There were a lot more dinosaurs charging down Main Street. At this rate, there really was going be a showdown at high noon. Except there wasn't gonna be much he and Charge could do against all these giant dinos.

"Well, I hope you're happy," Josh cried. "At least you'll be nice and rich, while the rest of us have to move to a different county."

The judge sat bolt upright in his seat. His normally icy-blue eyes turned red around the edges with fury. "That's enough of that, young man. I won't have you besmirch my good name any longer. Sheriffs, seize him!"

But before the officials in the courtroom had a chance to do anything, there was another huge rumble. This time, one of the giant stego-sauruses had parked itself right by the build-ing. Fear turned everyone quiet.

Josh rushed to the window. This time when he peered out, the stegosaurus was right outside. Even Josh, a pretty fearless dino rider, felt a little nervous. The stego lowered its neck, and its giant, yellow-green pupil seemed to fill the size of the window. It blinked a long, slow blink, its eyelashes rubbing up against the pane like it was a window cleaner.

Suddenly, though, the stegosaurus jumped back. It caught the reflection of itself in the pane of glass and didn't seem to like what it saw.

"So that's it," Josh said under his breath. "Stegosauruses aren't scared of water. The dumb dinos are scared of their own reflections!"

"Wow." Sam laughed. "Those dinos really are dumb."

"Yeah, but they are kinda scary," Abi said. "No wonder they're frightened!"

The stegosaurus outside wasn't done being

scared. It reared backward from the building. Its rider seemed totally unable to control it. It careened out into the street, then the huge dino came stumbling back toward the courthouse like it was slip-sliding on ice. With a huge thud, the stegosaurus began bashing into the side of the building. The lights fell from the wall, and the room descended into chaos. Even scary old Judge Coldbody looked fearful.

Abi and Sam looked around, wide-eyed. If they didn't do something fast, the stegosaurus was going to demolish the building—with them in it!

Josh leapt into action. He wasn't the local dino rider hero for nothing. He grabbed his lasso from his belt and jumped on a table.

The Wildest, Wackiest Laws in the Lost Plains

Local man Walter Matty was once imprisoned for two days for impersonating a hot dog.

Clipping a dinosaur's toenail carries a fine of $12.50.

Parking a dinosaur on Main Street is not allowed between the hours of 7:00 p.m. and 9:00 p.m.

It's illegal to have a sleeping dinosaur in your bathtub before 6:00 a.m. (After that is fine.)

Once he was up high, he began to call out to the room.

"Everyone, follow me," he said as more bits of ceiling and wall fell all around them. "This stego is a real bruiser. It's time to get outta here!"

CHAPTER 7

Josh gripped his lasso tight and snapped it against the ground. It cracked like a clap of thunder.

"Everybody, run!" he shouted loudly. "Get out of here!"

The courtroom hummed with activity as crooks and visitors alike piled out of the building. Even Judge Coldbody rose from his seat and scuttled around his desk. He practically flew out of the building, screaming as he went. Josh hurried people out the door as quickly as he could. He, Sam, and Abi were the last to leave.

"What do we do?" Sam asked.

Ahead of them, the stegosaurus was butting into the courthouse building, shaking the foundations. Glass and wood were flying everywhere, and people on Main Street had to take cover.

Josh stepped out into the street. Above him, the stegosaurus roared and swung its huge spiky tail in his direction. He quickly ducked and dodged to avoid being pounded to a pulp by the huge beast. The dino's foot stomped downward, narrowly missing Josh's head. Up above, the rider struggled with the dinosaur's reins, but eventually, he managed to calm the beast down just enough to get it under control. The stegosaurus went charging down the street in the other direction.

"Whoa!" Abi gasped. "Just wait 'til noon when there are twenty of those things charging down the street. What are we gonna do then?"

"It's the reflections," Josh said. "That's what they're scared of. When Wilks arrives with the

full stegosaurus building crew, that's what we hit them with. We need to get everyone on board. The whole town needs to be involved."

"And how do we do that?" Sam asked.

"We round 'em up like iguanodons on the plains. C'mon, guys, let's go!"

Together, Josh, Sam, and Abi untied their dinos from where they were tethered. Josh jumped on Charge, Abi and Sam on Fire and Nickel. They charged up and down the length of Main Street as quickly as they could. Josh had a plan. It would take everyone in Trihorn to put it into place, but if it worked, it meant that the town would be saved. It was less than two hours until high noon. Josh, Sam, and Abi didn't have time to lose.

Stegosaurus Profile

Weighs 5 to 7 tons fully grown

Between 17 and 22 bony plates attached to their skin

Scared of their own reflections

Spiky tail—called a "thagomizer"—for smashing and impaling

The huge town clock ticked ever closer to noon. The sun was rising high in the sky. Shadows were shrinking and tempers were fraying as the midday heat swept across Trihorn. However, the three friends stood firm, alongside the residents of Main Street.

Josh walked out in front of the assembled crowd. "All right, folks," he said. "This is it. Our one chance to get rid of these stegosauruses and save Trihorn. Be ready on my mark."

Sam and Abi stood at the front of the crowd too, firm resolve in their eyes.

"Let's do this," said Sam.

"Yeah," Abi agreed. "Let's stop mean Wilks's plan for good."

"Once we're done," said Sam, "he won't know what hit him!"

A loud chime rang out, clanging across the Lost Plains. The town clock had just struck twelve. High noon. Josh looked ahead expectantly. At first, there was just heat haze on the horizon. But sure enough, a couple of seconds later, something rumbled its way over the hill.

"This is it, guys," Josh said. Over the horizon, a large group of stegosauruses stomped their way toward Trihorn. "Get ready!"

What seemed like an army of dino brutes kicked up dust as they trampled their way

into town. Huge clouds seemed to blot out the light. The windows in the buildings lining Main Street rattled, and the wooden struc-tures shook. Sure enough, the dinosaurs were led by the spindly, mean figure of Malachi Wilks. A crooked smile danced across his face as he approached. When he stopped, he stepped down from his angry-looking anky-losaur, leather boots landing harshly on the ground. He stared at Josh with a mean glint in his beady eyes.

Josh reckoned Main Street had never been so busy. Behind him were Sam and Abi and at least a hundred residents. In front of him were Malachi Wilks, his corrupt judge, Coldbody, and around twenty giant stegosauruses and their riders. Even though it was busy, everyone was deadly quiet. Tumbleweeds blew across the main road.

"OK, partner," Wilks said with a smirk. "Time's up. It's high noon, and here I am, as promised. You could've just left Trihorn like the rest of those schmucks, but no, you had to stay on and be a hero."

Josh fumed. The crowd grew uneasy behind him. "First of all," he began, "I ain't your partner. And second, I *am* a hero. A Trihorn hero."

Coldbody sniggered. "Don't matter if you're a hero, not when we got the law on our side."

"Yeah," Wilks agreed. "There's gonna be a railroad through this town, and there's nothing you can do to stop it. If you lot don't get out of the way, the stegosauruses will just have to bulldoze you too."

At this, Josh let a smile of his own creep across his face. "And how are you going to have a railroad come through this town," he said, "when you don't have any dinosaurs to lug the metal or any workers to lay the tracks?"

Wilks's forehead creased in confusion. He swatted at the greasy hair that fell over his face. "What you talkin' about, boy? Can't you see how many dinosaurs I got behind me?"

"I can," Josh said. "But can't you see what I've got behind me?" Josh gestured to the people behind him.

"Uh, yeah," said Wilks. "I see them. But you know, those stegosauruses could make a flat

pancake outta all these Trihorn folks. I don't see what they got to do with anything."

"Well, see this," Josh said. "There ain't gonna be no stegosauruses flattening us. 'Cause really, they're just big old scaredy-cats."

He gave the signal, and there was a flurry of activity. Sam, Abi, and all the other residents rummaged around and pulled out reflective surfaces from bags or from inside coats or from under great big sheets. Everyone had something, a handheld mirror or a large wall mirror.

"Now watch this," said Josh.

CHAPTER
8

Wilks still had a frown of confusion on his face when the first of the stegosauruses took fright. Confronted with their reflections, the stegosauruses lifted their huge necks and let out cries of fear into the air.

"What in the world of the Lost Plains?" Wilks gasped.

The front line of stegosauruses reacted just as Josh knew they would. Faced with their own ugly faces, they panicked and started to back down Main Street. The crowd jeered, but it wasn't over yet.

Josh urged them onward. "Forward march!" he yelled.

The crowd surged forward, holding up their mirrors and reflective surfaces. The stegosauruses reared backward in fright.

"That's it," yelled Sam. "It's working!"

Sure enough, more and more of the dinosaurs were turning on their giant heels. Once a few of them had gotten scared and left, the rest of their herd instinct kicked in. All they could do was follow the others. They all turned and fled down Main Street, heading right out of Trihorn altogether.

"Hey, you!" Wilks shouted in vain. "Get back here!" But it was no use. No amount of shouting was going to make a herd of stegosauruses turn around once they got going.

A cheer erupted from the Trihorners.

"We did it!" Abi cried.

"Yes!" Sam shouted. "Take that, Wilks!"

Malachi Wilks looked as if his head was about to explode in frustration.

"You lot don't understand," Wilks said through gritted teeth. "It doesn't matter what you sniveling little children do. I'll just get even more stegosauruses. I'll get a T. rex. I'll get any dinosaur it takes until this town is mine and my railroad gets built!"

Just then, Josh spotted another figure on

the horizon. He didn't know who it could be, since most of Trihorn's townsfolk were right there. But then he realized—it was none other than Judge Mathers, returning from his holiday. He casually approached on his lazy-looking gallimimus, looking tanned and relaxed. He was even wearing a colorful shirt and a funny hat, like he'd just been to one great big beach party.

"Well, howdy, folks," he said as he ambled up to the crowd. "What did I miss?"

There was silence all around. Buildings had been destroyed. Practically everyone who lived on Main Street was milling about. Josh would say that the judge had missed quite a lot. Everyone began talking at once until Mathers had to turn stern and judge-y and tell them all to be quiet.

"One at a time, folks!" he barked.

As quickly as they could, Josh, Sam, and Abi filled the judge in on all the recent events. Looking up at the barrel-chested, mustachioed judge, Wilks and Coldbody didn't seem quite as mean and confident as they had been. In fact, they began to look downright scared. Mathers made them hand over the contract Mayor Dorkins had signed, saying that Wilks owned the town, so he could see for himself what was going on.

"See," Josh said. "We had to stop him."

"Well," Judge Mathers began. "That's about the biggest, smelliest, rottenest pile of dino dung I ever heard of."

Josh frowned. He wasn't sure which bit Mathers meant—the railroad or the fact that they had tried to stop it.

"There ain't no way in the Lost Plains that any one man can own Trihorn, let alone build a railway through it."

The Trihorners let out a cheer.

"In fact, that man should be arrested for even thinking it, let alone swindlin' you people all this time! Sheriffs," Mathers demanded, "take this man away."

Two burly men grabbed Wilks by the arms and led him away.

"Nooo," he wailed. "You can have anything you want...gold, jewels...a nice ranch... anything. I didn't do anything wrong!"

But it was no good. Wilks was hauled off in the direction of the county jail. Judge Coldbody tried to back away, but the crowd wasn't having any of it and made sure to stop him in his tracks. As they did so, an envelope fell right out of his pocket, and hundreds of dino dollar bills flew everywhere.

"And take him too!" Mathers demanded. "He's just as crooked as the other one. No lawman should have allowed this to go ahead. He's obviously a crook! Neither of them will set foot in this town ever again!"

Judge Coldbody squealed as the sheriffs led him away. But no one doubted it any more— he'd clearly been bribed by Malachi Wilks. Both of them were gonna be going to jail for a long time, and they wouldn't be posing any problems for Trihorn anymore. The railroad project was finished.

Josh, Sam, and Abi beamed with delight.

"And what do we do with all this money?" Sam asked. The residents were grabbing as much of it as they could before it blew off down the street.

Mathers thought for a moment, then declared, "Well, it seems to me that Trihorn has got a bit of rebuilding to do, doesn't it? Those shady villains managed to knock down a couple of buildings before you brave young 'uns stopped them. So how about we put the money toward that?"

The three friends and the other residents

all agreed. The kids got some hearty slaps on the back from the townsfolk whose livelihoods were saved.

"As long as there's no more railroad," Josh said and laughed.

"Don't worry, son," said Mathers. "There's no chance of that!"

Together, Josh, Sam, and Abi collected their dinosaurs and made their way back down Main Street as the cleanup operation began. Their smiles stretched from ear to ear.

"I could get used to this," said Sam.

"What's that?" asked Abi.

"Oh, you know, us three, constantly saving Trihorn from dinosaurs and mean villains."

Josh laughed. He reckoned the three of

them weren't half-bad dino riders and Trihorn protectors.

"I think you're right," Josh said, holding on tight to his lasso as Charge trundled down the street. "Hungry dinosaurs and mean villains oughta watch out when we're around!"

ABOUT THE AUTHOR

Ever since he was a little boy, Will Dare has been mad about T. rexes and velociraptors. He always wondered what it would be like to live in a world where they were still alive. Now, grown up, he has put pen to paper and imagined just that world. Will lives in rural America with his wife and his best pal, Charge (a dog, not a triceratops).

See where the adventure began!

How to Tame a Triceratops

Book 1

It was 8:00 a.m., and Josh Sanders was sitting on a dinosaur.

This wasn't unusual. He sat on a dinosaur almost every morning. In fact, most people in the Lost Plains did. But Josh had been in his saddle for a while now, and his butt was beginning to ache.

"Plodder," Josh moaned as he wriggled in his seat. "You're about as comfy as a cactus!"

Plodder kicked his feet and snorted into the air. A gooey trail of dino snot splattered onto the ground.

"Ew!" Josh laughed. "And you're gross!" He gave the gallimimus a friendly pat on the side. "C'mon, buddy. We've got iguanodons to find. We can't sit around here all day!"

Josh made a clicking noise with his mouth and nudged the dinosaur with the heel of his boot. Slowly, he began to move forward. In the distance, Josh could see the huge fence that kept the predators out. Well, most of them. No fence this side of the Lost Plains could keep out a T. rex.

"Come on, Plod," he urged, rocking in the saddle. "Sometimes, I think it'd be quicker if *I* carried *you*!"

Plodder was a long-necked, reliable gallimimus, used for herding iguanodons—but he was getting old now. Josh would do anything for a faster dino. His hero, Terrordactyl Bill, rode around on a triceratops, protecting the Lost Plains from fearsome dinosaurs and criminals. He was the greatest dino rider ever. Legend had it he'd once knocked out a brontosaurus with a single punch. Josh smiled at the thought of T-Bill in action. Now *that* would be an exciting life.

Eventually, Josh spotted the group of iguanodons he was after. They were wandering near the edge of the Sanders' Ranch territory, right where the predators roamed. It was Josh's job to herd them back where they belonged. With their bulky bodies and lumbering walk,

iguanodons weren't the fastest dinosaurs, but they sure could beat you up if you didn't treat them right.

"OK, Plodder," he cried. "It's time for some action!"

Unclipping the rope from his belt, Josh gave it a twirl above his head.

Ker-ack!

Josh snapped the lasso like a whip in the air behind the iguanodons. At once, a deep roar went up from the herd, and the beasts broke into a run.

"Now we're talking. Let's go!"

As Josh yanked on the reins, Plodder hollered and set off in pursuit. Josh felt the ground shake as the heavy iguanodon herd grunted and snorted, thundering across the plains and back toward the ranch. As the sun rose above the Wandering Mountains in the distance, he let out a whoop of joy.

"Woo-hoo!" he yelled, raising the rope above his head once more. His hat flew backward, and he felt the wind whistling through his sandy hair. Sometimes, riding Plodder wasn't so bad after all!

He moved toward the iguanodons, gently steering them in the right direction and dodging in and out of their gigantic legs and stinky bodies. However, as most of the iguanodons made their way back toward their pen, Josh suddenly noticed one of the big brutes veering off from the herd.

How to Rope a Giganotosaurus

Book 2

DINO RIDERS

How to Rope a Giganotosaurus

Will Dare

How to Hog-Tie a T-Rex

Book 3

How to Catch a Dino Thief

Book 4

How to Track a Pterodactyl

Book 5

DINO RIDERS
How to Track a Pterodactyl

Will Dare